Chapter One
WISHES

Ali raced to answer the phone.

"Hello, Birthday Girl!" said Grandma when she heard Ali's voice.

"My birthday isn't until next week," Ali reminded her.

"I'm trying to think of a super duper present," said Grandma. "Any hints?"

Ali hesitated. "You know what I want most, Grandma?"

"Oh, sweetie." Grandma sounded sad. "You know you can't have a cat. Not with Jay's allergies."

For a moment, Ali had dared to hope. But what was the use? Her big brother, Jay, was allergic to cats,

1

so they couldn't have a cat in the house. Not ever. And that was that.

"I have an idea," said Grandma. "Let's go birthday shopping together. How about Thursday? I'll be back from my trip by then."

"Oh, yes, Grandma!" said Ali. Her spirits lifted a bit. Shopping with Grandma was so fun.

"I'll see you then," said Grandma.

"Have fun at Auntie Claire's," said Ali, and she hung up the phone.

"Leelee!" Ali turned. Her baby brother, Ben, stumbled up the hall toward her.

Ali gasped. Ben had her favorite necklace. It was made of brightly colored beads, like jewels a queen would wear. It was so long Ali could wind it three times around her neck.

Ali jumped to her feet. "Ben, give me my necklace. Right now!" she shouted.

Too late. Ben tripped on the necklace. The string broke. Beads flew in all directions. Ben fell down and began to wail.

Mom hurried from the kitchen. "What happened?" she asked, picking Ben up.

Ali scrambled after the beads. "He broke my necklace." She glared at Ben. "He's always taking my things."

Mom soothed Ben. "I'm sorry about your necklace, Ali," she said. "But we can fix it."

"I wish he would leave my things alone," Ali said crossly.

"Ben didn't mean any harm," Mom said. "Come on. Let's have some juice."

In the kitchen, Mom put Ben into his high chair. Ben peeked around her at Ali. His tear-streaked face broke into a grin. Ali grinned back. It was hard to stay cross with Ben.

Mom poured juice into glasses for Ali and herself. She poured juice into a sippy cup for Ben. The sippy cup had cats drawn all around the sides.

"That was my sippy cup," Ali said.

"You don't use it anymore," said Mom.

Ben banged the sippy cup on his high chair.

Ali sighed. "I hope he doesn't break it," she said.

Mom smiled. "I think it's break proof."

Ali told Mom about Grandma's phone call. "We're going birthday shopping on Thursday," she said.

"That sounds exciting," said Mom. She lifted Ben from his high chair. "It's time for your nap, mister."

Ali followed Mom and Ben upstairs. She went to her own room. The shelf over her bed was filled with cats. There were big cats on the shelf. There were little cats on the shelf. Some were made of glass and some were made of china. Others were made of soft fuzzy cloth. They all had names. There was Bernadette and Grumpuss, Chloe and Gina, Catfish and Julia, and Chacha and Mr. Bumbles. Ali loved her cat collection. But she wished, oh, how she wished, that just one of them was a real live cat.

Ali sat on her bed. She picked up Tedward Bear. "I wish I had a big brother who wasn't allergic to cats," she whispered in his ear. "I wish I had a baby

brother who didn't take my things." She hugged Tedward Bear. "But most of all, I wish I could have a real cat of my very own."

Chapter Two
A SPECIAL PLACE

The next afternoon, Ali played at her best friend Sam's house.

Sam had two cats. One was black and white. His name was Panda. Sam's other cat had gray stripes. Her name was Lucy.

Panda lay down beside Ali. He rolled onto his back. Ali rubbed his tummy. Panda purred loudly.

"I wish I had a cat like you," Ali said.

"Maybe I can give you one for your birthday," said Sam.

"We can't have a cat in our house," Ali reminded him.

Sam frowned. "I forgot your brother's allergic." Then he grinned. "You can play with Panda and Lucy any time you're here."

But it wasn't the same as having a cat of her own. Ali didn't say that out loud though. It would be rude.

Sam's mom looked in the doorway. "Samuel," she said, "it's garbage day tomorrow. You haven't cleaned the litterboxes."

"I'll do it later," said Sam.

"Now, please," said his mom. "You might forget later." Sam had a habit of forgetting things he didn't like to do.

Sam stood up. "Do you want to help?" he asked Ali.

Ali wrinkled her nose. Litterboxes were stinky. But Sam was her best friend. "I'll help," she said, "but not the stinky part."

Ali held the garbage bag while Sam dumped in the smelly litter. Then he washed the boxes.

Ali filled them with fresh litter. "Can we feed Panda and Lucy now?" she asked.

"Sure," said Sam. He got a tin of cat food from the cupboard. When the cats heard the can opener, they came running.

Lucy rubbed around Ali's ankles. Ali picked her up. Her fur was so soft, like Ben's baby blanket.

Lucy smelled food. She struggled in Ali's arms.

Ali put her down. Just in time. Panda had already gobbled his food. Now he headed for Lucy's. Lucy hissed at him. She did not want to share her food.

"Let's go play in the yard," Ali said. Sam's yard was a neat place. There were swings and slides. There were big tubes to run through. There were bars to hang upside down from and ropes to climb.

For the rest of the afternoon, Sam and Ali climbed and swung and slid and ran races.

On Monday, Sam came to Ali's house for the day. "Let's play in the clubhouse," he said.

Ali's backyard was larger than Sam's. The bottom end was overgrown with bushes and trees. Hidden among the trees was the clubhouse. To Ali it was the most special place in the whole world.

Chapter Three
SOMETHING'S IN THE BUSHES!

When Ali's family first moved into their house, her dad wanted to pull out the bushes and trees and plant a garden. But Ali and Jay had begged him to leave it the way it was.

"The bushes are neat for hiding in," Jay said.

"We can fix up the shed like a clubhouse," Ali added.

Ali and Jay cleaned out the shed. But being in the shed made Jay's allergies worse. He couldn't play there at all.

"Can it be mine?" Ali asked. "Just mine?"

"I don't see why not," Dad answered. He put a screen in one window to let in fresh air. He made a new door and put up some shelves. Mom gave Ali an old rug and a couple of comfortable chairs and a table.

When it was finished, it was the neatest clubhouse Ali had ever seen. And it was all hers. Only she and Sam ever played in it.

Mom made Sam and Ali a jug of lemonade. She gave them a bag of homemade granola. Ali licked her lips. Mom's homemade granola was yummy.

On the way to the clubhouse, Ali sneaked the almonds out of the granola. Almonds were her favorite.

Sam noticed. "No fair," he protested. "You're eating all the good stuff so you don't have to share."

Ali looked guilty. She handed the bag to Sam. He rooted around until he found two almonds Ali had missed. He gobbled them up quickly.

"What do you want to do today?" Ali asked when they reached the clubhouse. It was very warm inside, so she opened both windows.

"Let's be adventurers," said Sam. "In the jungle. We can track big game." Sam had heard that on a TV program. He thought it sounded cool.

They went back outside. There was a narrow dirt path between the bushes. Ali and Sam had to crawl on their hands and knees.

Sam led the way. "Ali," he shouted suddenly. "Look, tracks!"

Ali looked over his shoulder. In a muddy spot beside the path, there were small footprints. "All right!" Ali cheered. "Let's follow them."

Farther on, the bushes gave way to small trees. Now they could walk upright.

Suddenly, Sam stopped. "Hey," Ali protested, almost falling over him.

"Sh-h-h-h," Sam hissed. "I saw something."

"What?" Ali whispered.

"I think it was some kind of a wild creature," Sam whispered back.

Ali gulped. This was more adventure than she wanted. "Maybe we'd better go back to the clubhouse," she said.

"Yes." Sam turned around. "Not that I'm scared or anything."

"Me neither," Ali spoke up quickly.

As they hurried back to the clubhouse, Ali kept glancing over her shoulder. Was that footsteps she heard thumping behind them? Or was it just her heart pounding?

When they were safely inside, Ali breathed a sigh of relief. "Do you want to play Monopoly?" she asked.

"Okay," said Sam.

Ali got out the game box. It was old and raggedy. Most of the money was missing. But the game was safe and familiar, like the clubhouse. Still, as Ali threw the dice, little prickles of fear jabbed at her. What had Sam seen hiding in the bushes?

Chapter Four

A SURPRISE VISITOR

When she woke the next morning, Ali propped Tedward Bear on her stomach.

"Sam's gone to his dad's," she told him. "Kim and Nav are away too. Jay's at camp. There's no one to play with." Tedward Bear didn't say anything, but Ali knew he felt sorry for her.

Ali heard Mom and Ben in the kitchen. She pulled on shorts and a T-shirt and ran downstairs.

"Leelee!" Ben greeted her from his high chair. His face was sticky with honey and toast crumbs.

Mom looked up from the list she was writing. "Good morning, sleepyhead," she said.

"G'morning," said Ali as she poured herself a bowl of cereal.

"Me! Me! Me!" Ben shouted.

Ali shook some cereal onto Ben's tray.

Mom put the list in her purse. "We're going grocery shopping this morning," she said.

Boring! Ali thought as she munched her cereal.

But Ali was wrong. The shopping trip was not boring.

On the way to the store, Ben emptied a whole box of Kleenex onto the backseat. At the store, he shouted "Hi, me Bennie!" to everyone they met. People laughed. They thought he was cute. Ali thought he was embarrassing.

On the way home, they stopped for ice cream. They sat outside at a picnic table so Ben wouldn't make a mess in the car. Soon Ben's face was covered with ice cream. Again people laughed. Again, Ali felt embarrassed.

When they got home, Ali helped Mom put the groceries away. Mom put the fresh salmon she had bought into a casserole dish. She put it in the oven.

"We'll have salmon salad for dinner tonight," she said.

"Yum," said Ali. Salmon salad was one of her favorites.

After lunch, Ali said, "I'm going to play in the clubhouse."

"All by yourself?" asked Mom.

Ali's face lit up. "Can you come too?" she asked.

"I wish I could," Mom said. "But it's time for Ben's nap. I can't leave him alone in the house."

Ali slouched out the back door. "Ben, Ben, Ben," she muttered. "Mom's always busy with Ben." Today, Ali really wanted company. But there was no one around. Even the sun had gone behind the clouds.

When she got to the clubhouse, her spirits lifted. "This is the best place in the whole world," she said out loud. "And it's just mine."

A slight breeze ruffled Ali's hair. She looked up. Uh-oh, she had left both of the windows open overnight. Luckily it hadn't rained.

Ali sat, chin in hand, thinking about what she could do by herself. She could play Monopoly or Crazy Eights or Go Fish. But games aren't any fun when you have to play them alone.

Ali noticed her paint box sitting on the table. That's what she could do. She could paint a picture for Grandma. Grandma loved Ali's paintings.

Ali jumped up to get her paints. Suddenly she froze. Her heart pounded. Behind a box in the corner, something moved.

Chapter Five
PROMISES

The wild creature Sam saw yesterday…it was right here in the clubhouse! The open windows caught Ali's eye. That's how the creature had gotten in. Ali wanted to run, but her feet weren't listening.

Something darted out from behind the box. Ali gasped. Then she let out a shriek of delight. The creature was a cat!

"Meow," said the cat.

Ali stared. It was the most beautiful cat she had ever seen. Her eyes were jewel green. Her nose looked like a small pink button. She was white from head to toe, like freshly fallen snow in winter.

"If you were my cat," Ali whispered, "I'd call you Snowy."

The cat ran to her. She circled Ali's ankles, purring loudly.

Ali crouched down. "Snowy," she repeated, "do you like that name?"

"Meow," said Snowy.

Ali ran her hand along Snowy's back. "Where did you come from?" she asked.

Snowy didn't answer. She lay down and rolled over. Bits of dried grass clung to her tummy. Her paws were very dirty.

Ali picked off the dried grass. She spit on a Kleenex and washed Snowy's paws. "I'll bet you don't have a home," said Ali. Snowy stood up. She put her front paws on Ali's knee. "Meow," she said. The meow sounded lost and lonely.

That's when Ali had a wonderful idea. "You can live here, Snowy!" she said. "I can bring you food and water every day." The words tumbled from her mouth.

"I'll play with you and make you a special bed." She hugged Snowy gently. "You can be my cat. My very own cat."

Snowy struggled out of Ali's arms. She ran to the door and meowed. "Oh, Snowy, I can't let you out," Ali said. "You might get lost again. You'll be safe in here."

Snowy wasn't listening. She paced back and forth. What was the matter?

Ali scrambled to her feet. "I'll bet you're hungry," she said. "I'll get you some food and water. Right now. And I'll play with you all afternoon."

When she went to the door, Snowy wanted to come too.

"You can't come into the house," Ali said. "My brother Jay is allergic." She started to explain what allergic meant. Then she stopped. It might hurt Snowy's feelings.

Ali was almost out the door when she remembered the windows. Both were open. Only one had a screen in it. Snowy couldn't get out the screened window. But she could get out the other one. Ali hurried over and closed that one tightly. Snowy still had plenty of fresh air, but she could not get outside.

Ali rushed to her house. What could she feed Snowy? She didn't have any cat food. She had to find something. Snowy was hungry.

When Ali came into the kitchen, she saw the baked salmon cooling on the counter. Cats love salmon, thought Ali. But she couldn't just take the salmon. Mom would ask what happened to it. And she couldn't tell Mom about Snowy.

Ali stared at the salmon. There was a lot of it. She looked into the den. Mom was working at the computer. Ali leaned over Mom's shoulder. "Can I make myself a salmon sandwich?" she asked.

Mom looked up. "You just had lunch," she said.

"I'm still hungry," said Ali.

"Okay," said Mom.

"Can I eat it in the clubhouse?" Ali asked.

Mom nodded. "But come right back. As soon as Ben wakes up from his nap, I'm taking you both for a haircut."

Ali groaned. "Mom, I don't need a haircut," she protested.

"You really do," Mom answered. She ran her hand over Ali's thick dark curls.

Ali's heart sank. She would not be able to play with Snowy this afternoon after all.

Chapter Six
KEEPING SNOWY

Ali didn't put any butter on the salmon sandwich. She didn't put any mayonnaise on the sandwich either. That might not be good for Snowy.

She grabbed two bowls from the cupboard. She grabbed a bottle of water from the fridge. She shouted good-bye to Mom and raced back to the clubhouse.

Ali scraped the salmon into one of the bowls. She saved the bread and one small bit of salmon for herself.

As soon as Snowy smelled the salmon, she began to meow. Her pink nose twitched. She meowed and meowed.

Ali put the bowl down, and Snowy began to gobble. "Poor Snowy," Ali said. "You were so hungry."

She filled the other bowl with water and set it beside Snowy.

Ali munched her plain bread sandwich. She saved the bit of salmon for last. But before Ali got to it, Snowy's bowl was empty.

Snowy put her front paws on Ali's arm. "Meow," she said.

Ali held out the bit of salmon. Snowy licked it off her fingers. Her rough tongue tickled. Ali giggled. "I love you, Snowy," she said. She felt like the luckiest girl in the world. She now had a cat of her very own.

Ali heard Mom calling, "Ali, it's time to leave." She scrambled to her feet.

"I have to go now, Snowy," Ali said. "But I'll be back soon. I promise."

This time Ali was able to keep her promise. As soon as she got back from the hairdresser, she hurried to the clubhouse.

Snowy was right behind the door. Ali felt guilty.

Had Snowy been waiting by the door the whole time she was gone?

As Ali came in, she sniffed. She smelled salmon. She smelled something else too. Phe-ew! She noticed a small mound in the corner. Uh-oh.

Ali almost gagged as she cleaned up the poop. Snowy rubbed against her arm. Ali hugged her. "It's okay," she said. "It's not your fault. You need a litterbox."

Ali went to the garage. She looked until she found an old plastic dishpan. Nobody was using it. It would make a perfect litterbox. But what could she use for litter?

Sam put special litter stuff into Panda's and Lucy's litterboxes. It looked like clumpy sand. But I don't have any of that, Ali thought. Then she noticed Ben's sandbox in the yard. Ordinary sand would work. Ali scooped some dry sand into the dish pan. Perfect.

Back at the clubhouse, Ali showed Snowy her new litterbox. Ali felt very proud of herself.

Snowy had food. Snowy had fresh water. Snowy had a litterbox. What else did she need?

A bed, Ali thought. She ran back to the house. She raced up to her room. On the floor was her doll's wicker bed.

Ali dumped out the doll who was sleeping in it. She got her old baby blanket from her bottom drawer. It was worn thin, but it was soft and clean. It would make a cozy bed for Snowy.

For the rest of the afternoon, Ali played with Snowy. Snowy liked playing with string. She liked chasing Ali's tennis ball. She liked curling up on Ali's lap while Ali read to her.

Once in a while though, Snowy went and stood by the door. "Meow," she said. Was she saying, "Let me out"? Ali hoped not.

Chapter Seven
SECRETS

At dinner, Ali saved some chicken for Snowy. When no one was looking, she wrapped it in a napkin and shoved it into her pocket. She didn't like being sneaky. But what else could she do? She had to look after Snowy.

Late that night, Ali woke up. She thought about Snowy. Maybe Snowy was lonely. Maybe she was afraid of the dark.

Ali hugged Tedward Bear. He always made her feel better when she was lonely or afraid. Snowy wouldn't be lonely or afraid if she had Tedward Bear for company. Ali had never slept without Tedward Bear. But maybe Snowy needed him more than she did.

Ali scrambled out of bed. She grabbed her slippers. She grabbed her flashlight. She grabbed the chicken she had saved from dinner. And she grabbed Tedward Bear. She sneaked downstairs. She sneaked out the back door. She almost sneaked right back in again!

The yard was scary at night. Moon shadows crept across the lawn. Ali gulped. Her flashlight barely lit the path to the clubhouse. Her heart thumped. By the time she reached the door, her legs were shaking.

Ali shone her flashlight around. In the wicker bed, two eyes glowed like fireflies.

Ali tiptoed over and put Tedward Bear in the bed beside Snowy. She put the chicken into Snowy's dish.

"I'll see you tomorrow," Ali whispered. "Sleep tight." She kissed Snowy on her pink nose. She kissed Tedward Bear on his brown button nose.

Back outside, Ali stared into the dark. Was that something rustling in the bushes? Ali broke into a run. Bushes whacked at her. She stumbled and almost fell twice.

She opened the back door quietly and crept upstairs to bed. Even after she was safely under the covers, her heart still pounded. Her bedroom was as dark as a cave. She wished with all her might that she had Tedward Bear for company.

Snowy needs him more than I do, Ali told herself sternly. Still, it was a long time before she finally fell asleep.

When she woke the next morning, Ali made plans. She would spend the whole day with Snowy.

Ali thought of things they could do in the clubhouse. There weren't that many. If they could play in the yard, they could climb the maple tree. They could play hide-and-seek. They could have a picnic lunch. But she couldn't let Snowy out. Mom might see her. Snowy might get lost. Ali decided that they would have to play inside.

After breakfast, Mom said, "As soon as I get Ben changed, we'll go to the park."

"The park?" Ali groaned. "Do we have to go to the park?" she asked. "Can't we stay home?"

Mom looked surprised. "But you love going to the park," she said. She looked at Ali closely. "Are you not feeling well, sweetie?"

Maybe I can say I'm sick, Ali thought. But then Mom will make me stay in bed. Probably all day. "I feel okay," she said reluctantly.

While Mom got Ben ready, Ali raced to the clubhouse. She yanked the door open. Tedward Bear was lying on the floor. Snowy was not in her bed. Where could she be?

Chapter Eight
LOOKING AFTER SNOWY

"Meow."

Ali looked up. Her breath whooshed out in relief. Snowy looked down at her from the shelf above the window.

"What were you doing up there?" Ali asked as she reached for Snowy. Then her face went serious. "I have to go to the park this morning, Snowy. But I'll play with you all afternoon. Promise."

Snowy struggled out of Ali's arms. Ali bit her lip. Was Snowy cross with her? Then she saw Snowy's empty food dish. Snowy wasn't cross. She was hungry. And Ali hadn't brought any food for her.

Ali heard Mom calling. She sounded impatient.

"I have to go," she said. "But I'll be back soon. And I'll bring you food. And fresh water. Promise!"

As Ali moved toward the door, Snowy darted ahead of her. Ali had to close the door in Snowy's face. Sad little mews followed her along the path.

Ali thought of the promises she'd made to Snowy that she hadn't been able to keep. Her spirits sank. She did not enjoy the morning at the park.

When they stopped at the goldfish pond, Ben clapped his hands. "'ish! 'ish!" he shouted. Snowy would like the goldfish too, Ali thought.

Mom played ball with Ben. "Come play, Ali," she called.

Ali shook her head. Snowy would like playing ball too.

Thoughts tumbled through Ali's head. Her best wish had come true. She now had a cat of her very own. And she loved Snowy so much. So why did she feel sad? Ali wondered about that all the way home.

For lunch, Ali asked for a tuna sandwich. Mom looked in the cupboard. "Sorry, Ali, we're out of tuna," she said.

"Salmon?" Ali asked.

"I'm afraid we're out of that too," said Mom.

Ali looked in the fridge. She spotted a small bowl of leftover spaghetti and meatballs. Perfect. She and Snowy could share. Ali reached for the bowl. "Can I have this?" she asked.

"Yes," said Mom, "do you want me to heat it up for you?"

Ali shook her head. Snowy might not like hot food. "Can I eat at the clubhouse?" she asked.

Ben picked that moment to spill his milk on the floor. Mom grabbed a rag and began to mop. "Yes, okay," she said.

When Ali opened the clubhouse door, Snowy was waiting for her. Ali sniffed. In spite of the screened window being open, the room smelled stinky. But there were no messes on the floor. Snowy had used her litterbox.

"Good girl," said Ali. Snowy stood on her hind legs. She meowed and waved a paw in the air.

"I know," Ali said. "You're hungry. We'll eat lunch right now. Then I'll change your litterbox."

But Snowy did not like spaghetti. She did not like meatballs either.

"Snowy, you have to eat something," Ali pleaded. She mashed up a meatball and held it out on the end of her finger. Snowy turned up her little pink nose. She looked at Ali and meowed and meowed.

Ali knew that she had to find something for Snowy to eat. But where? And what?

Chapter Nine
LOST CAT!

Ali hurried back to the house. She heard splashing and giggling sounds from upstairs. Mom was giving Ben his bath.

"Mom, can I have a snack?" Ali shouted.

"No junk food," Mom called back. "Find something nutritious."

Ali looked in the fridge. There was nothing that Snowy would eat. She looked in a cupboard. Cereal, tea, coffee, crackers. Snowy would not like any of that either. She opened the next cupboard. Jars of baby food caught her eye. Some were chicken. Some were beef. Some were vegetables.

Perfect. Snowy would like chicken. Ali reached for a jar. Then she hesitated. But Mom had said that she could have a snack. A nutritious snack. Baby food was very nutritious. Ali grabbed the jar and raced back to the clubhouse.

"Snowy," she hooted, "look what I brought you!" She opened the jar. Snowy's pink nose twitched. She meowed and meowed.

Ali emptied half the jar into Snowy's dish. Snowy gobbled the food. She licked the bowl and looked for more.

"We have to save the rest," Ali said. She put the top back on the jar. There was just enough left for tomorrow. Ali wondered what she could feed Snowy after that. Taking the jar of baby food today was okay. Well, sort of. But she couldn't keep taking more. That would be like stealing.

Ali noticed that Snowy's water dish was almost empty. That wasn't a problem. She washed it at the outside tap and filled it with fresh water. Snowy's litterbox needed to be cleaned. That was a problem. How long could Ali keep taking sand from Ben's sandbox before someone noticed?

Snowy leaped up onto the windowsill of the open screened window. She rubbed against the screen, sniffing the fresh air. She looked at Ali and meowed. Ali felt sad all over again. But she could not let Snowy go out.

The next day was Thursday, the day Ali and Grandma were going birthday shopping. They were even going out to dinner afterward.

Before Ali left, she gave Snowy the rest of the baby food. She gave her clean water and cleaned the poop out of her litterbox. "I have to go shopping with Grandma today," Ali explained. "But tomorrow I'll spend the whole day with you. Promise." Ali crossed her fingers, hoping this was a promise she could keep.

When Grandma arrived, Ali was waiting.

"Let's go to the mall," Grandma suggested as she backed out of the driveway. "Have you thought about what you might like for your birthday?"

An idea flashed through Ali's head. Maybe she could ask Grandma to buy her cat food for her birthday. But then she would have to tell Grandma about Snowy, and she couldn't do that. "I'm not sure, Grandma," she said.

"No matter," said Grandma. "We'll look around until we find something special."

After a lot of looking, they finally found something special. It was a green sweatshirt. Green was Ali's favorite color. On the front were three cats. They were white, like Snowy. Ali loved the sweatshirt. She would wear it whenever she played with Snowy.

Grandma stopped in front of the grocery store. "I have to pick up a couple of things," she said. "Then we'll go out for dinner."

As they walked into the grocery store, a large notice board caught Ali's eye. She stopped so suddenly she

almost tripped over her feet. *LOST CAT* read one of the notices.

Below it was a picture of a cat. The cat in the picture was Snowy.

Chapter Ten
ALI DECIDES

Ali stared at the notice. There were some words she couldn't read. "Grandma, what does that say?" she asked.

Grandma looked where Ali was pointing. "'Loved pet,'" she read. "'Owner desperate. Please call Ruby Banks at 905-316-2204.'"

Ali followed Grandma around the store in a daze. She thought of Snowy, alone in the clubhouse. Was she missing Ali? Or was she missing her desperate owner? *Loved pet*. The words stung Ali's heart. Snowy was her loved pet now. It wasn't fair. It just wasn't fair.

On the way to the car, Grandma said, "You're lost in thought, Ali." Then she smiled. "You love Chinese food. Let's go to Shanghai Gardens for dinner."

Any other time, Ali would have jumped with joy. Shanghai Gardens was her favorite restaurant. She loved the bright colors. She loved the Chinese letters everywhere. Today it was all she could do to force her mouth into a smile. "Okay, Grandma," she said.

When their food arrived, Ali put a little rice and a lot of chicken chow mein onto her plate. She planned to save all the chicken pieces for Snowy.

Ali picked at her vegetables. She was thinking about Snowy. The clubhouse seemed like the perfect place for Snowy to live. But was it? If Snowy was happy there, why was she always trying to get out? And what about food? And fresh litter?

"Ali, you've hardly eaten a thing," Grandma said gently. "Is something wrong?"

Ali couldn't hold it in any longer. She took a deep breath. Words flew from her mouth as she told Grandma the whole story of Snowy.

Grandma put her hand on Ali's arm. "What do you think you should do now?" she asked.

A tear ran down Ali's cheek. "I have to give Snowy back," she said. "Right now." Ali knew she had to do it before she changed her mind.

"Good girl," said Grandma. "I'll get the waiter to box up our food. We can eat it later."

Ali watched the waiter box up everything, including the chicken pieces she had saved for Snowy. But now she wouldn't need them. She felt as though her heart was breaking into pieces. Why was it so hard to do the right thing?

Chapter Eleven
SHARING SNOWY

Grandma drove back to the grocery store so Ali could get down the owner's name and phone number. Then they bought a tin of cat food. Just one. Ali bit back her tears. One tin was all she would need because Snowy was going home.

Back at Ali's house, they found a note from Mom. *Dad, Ben and I have gone out for dinner. Be back soon,* the note read.

Ali led the way to the clubhouse.

"Oh, my," Grandma said when she saw Snowy. "She is a beauty. I can see why you named her Snowy."

"Would you hold her while I get her food?" Ali asked.

Snowy was happy in Grandma's arms until she heard the tin opening. Then she wiggled and squirmed. "Meow. Meow," she said.

Grandma put Snowy down. Snowy gulped her dinner. If I ate that quickly, Mom would scold, Ali thought. But she didn't scold Snowy. Snowy had waited a long time for her dinner.

Grandma looked at Ali. "Are you ready to take her back now?" she asked.

No! No! No! Ali protested silently. But she nodded her head. She knew that she had to give Snowy back to Mrs. Banks.

Grandma took her cell phone from her purse and called the number Ali had written down. "Ruby Banks just lives over on Bonnymeadow Road," she said when she had finished. She put her hand on Ali's shoulder. "She's so happy that we found Snowflake."

Snowflake? Snowy's real name was Snowflake? No wonder she seemed to recognize her name. Ali picked up Snowy. She hugged her as tightly as she could without hurting her. "I guess you won't ever be called Snowy again," she said sadly.

Snowy sat quietly on Ali's lap all the way to Mrs. Bank's house. She looked out the window. Ali wondered if Snowy knew she was going home.

When they turned onto Bonnymeadow Road, they didn't have to look for the house number. A lady was standing on the porch of the second house down. When she saw their car, she rushed to the curb.

"Snowflake!" she cried when she saw Snowy in Ali's arms.

Ali got out of the car. Maybe Mrs. Banks would scold her for keeping Snowy. Maybe she would be cross that Ali had given Snowy a new name.

Mrs. Banks didn't look cross. She was too busy smiling as Snowy jumped into her arms.

"We saw your Lost Cat notice in the supermarket," Grandma said.

"Where did you find her?" Mrs. Banks asked. "Snowflake got out accidentally. She's not an outdoor cat."

Ali told Mrs. Banks the whole story. "I'm sorry I kept her," she said in a small voice. "I just wanted to have a cat of my own. But I don't think she likes living in the clubhouse."

Mrs. Banks didn't scold. She didn't get cross. "Thank you for taking care of her," she said. "And most of all, thank you for bringing her back."

Ali bit back her tears. She reached over to give Snowy one last pat. "I'm going to miss you so much," she said. Snowy rubbed against Ali's hand.

"I think Snowflake will miss you too," said Mrs. Banks. "You could come and visit her," she added.

"Really, truly?" Ali gasped. "It will be like... sharing! I can help look after her. I can feed her and give her fresh water and play with her." The words tumbled from Ali's mouth. "I can even change her litterbox." Ali cupped her hands around Snowy's face. "Did you hear that? I'm going to come and visit you, Snowy." She stopped and looked at Mrs. Banks. "I mean, Snowflake."

Mrs. Banks smiled. "Maybe we can call her Snowy for short," she said.

Ali felt as though she could jump over the moon with joy. She didn't care if she got any other birthday presents. Sharing Snowy was the best present of all.

MARILYN HELMER is the author of many children's books, including picturebooks, early readers, novels and retold tales. She is a cat lover and enjoys writing stories about them. The quirks and antics of her own pet cats have provided her with some great ideas. Feisty Star, who lived to be twenty years old, was the inspiration for *Mr. McGratt and the Ornery Cat.* The tale of a stray named Tiger is told in the award-winning *Fog Cat.* Marilyn is now back with another cat story, *Sharing Snowy.* But this time the inspiration came not from a cat but from…a mouse!

Sharing Snowy is Marilyn's second book with Orca. Her first is *Dinosaurs on the Beach,* an Orca Young Reader published in 2003. Marilyn and her husband, Gary, share their home near Fergus, Ontario, with Misty, who rules the household with an iron paw.